10p

For Tom Powell –
who loves exploring. S.M.
For Baggins. T.M.

ORCHARD BOOKS
96 Leonard Street, London EC2A 4XD
Orchard Books Australia
32/45-51 Huntley Street, Alexandria, NSW 2015
ISBN 1 84362 563 6 (hardback)
ISBN 1 84362 571 7 (paperback)
First published in Great Britain in 2005
First paperback publication in 2006
Text © Sue Mongredien 2005
Illustrations © Teresa Murfin 2005
The rights of Sue Mongredien to be identified as the author
and of Teresa Murfin to be identified as the illustrator of this work
have been asserted by them in accordance with the
Copyright, Designs and Patents Act, 1988.
A CIP catalogue record for this book is available
from the British Library.
1 3 5 7 9 10 8 6 4 2 (hardback)
1 3 5 7 9 10 8 6 4 2 (paperback)
Printed in Great Britain
www.wattspublishing.co.uk

FRIGHTFUL FAMILIES

EXPLORER TRAUMA

SUE MONGREDIEN • TERESA MURFIN

ORCHARD BOOKS

Indiana Brown was born in a tent, deep in a tropical rainforest, while parrots squawked in the trees above.

A year later, he took his first steps at the top of Mount Everest.

Soon after that, he said his first word.

"Kangaroo!"

When he was two, Indiana learned to swing with monkeys on jungle vines.

By the time he was three, he was swimming with dolphins in the Indian Ocean.

But when he was four, his nan put her foot down. "Little Indiana needs to go to school," she told his mum and dad. "It's time you stopped dragging him around the world."

You didn't argue with Indiana's nan.
She was fiercer than any tiger.

She could glare like a cobra...

She could snap like a crocodile...

But she was always a pussycat to Indiana.

So, for the last four years, Indiana and his parents had been living next door to Nan. They tried to live a normal life but it wasn't easy. They weren't exactly *normal* people. Mr and Mrs Brown were explorers who had travelled the world.

They had hiked through steamy jungles...

They had scaled snow-capped mountains...

They had dived through crashing waterfalls and rafted down crocodile-infested rivers.

Most excitingly of all, they had discovered ancient treasures in long-forgotten temples.

All the other children at school thought that Indiana was the luckiest boy alive. He'd had more adventures than they could ever dream of.

But having explorer parents wasn't always so great.

Take breakfast. Mr and Mrs Brown didn't eat toast or cereal in the morning. Oh, no. They liked to catch their food themselves, the way they did in the rainforest. They called it "bushtucker".

Indiana called it "earthworms". Or "beetles". Or sometimes even "plants".

It was no wonder he stopped off at his
nan's house on the way to school. She made
the best bacon sandwiches in Britain.

Food wasn't the only problem. Mr
and Mrs Brown always wanted to go to
exciting places in the school holidays.

"Christmas in Peru?" Indiana's best friend,
Joe, would sigh. "Cool!"

"It won't be cool," Indiana would moan.
"It'll be boiling."

Indiana didn't really like hot weather. He got sunburn and prickly heat and sweaty knees. He didn't like snakes or spiders or cockroaches either.

He couldn't stand camping and he loathed flying on aeroplanes.

But the thing he hated most of all was that he missed his nan. "I wish we could just go to the seaside with you," he said to her every summer.

And every time, his nan would sigh and stroke his hair. "I wish you could, too, Indiana," she would say.

It was almost the end of term and Indiana's school were having a summer fair. There was a bouncy castle and a face-painting stand. There were games and a raffle. There were stalls selling toys and books and cakes. Mr and Mrs Brown could hardly wait to try everything.

Mrs Brown decided to have a go at the apple bobbing game first. "After catching sea-slugs with my teeth for lunch, this will be a doddle!" she said. Then she unzipped her rucksack, whipped out a snorkel and mask, and slapped them onto her face.

BUBBLE. BUBBLE. BUBBLE went
the snorkel.

"She's *cheating*!" cried a little girl loudly.
"That lady is CHEATING!"

"I say, Mrs Brown, stop that at once!" said
Mr Chinfluff, the teacher in charge.

But Indiana's mum didn't hear. She had pushed the snorkel out of her mouth and was gripping an apple stalk with her teeth.

"Bravo!" Mr Brown cheered.
"I'll have that back, thank you very much," Mr Chinfluff said crossly.

"Mum, you can't use a mask in the water. It's cheating," Indiana said in a low voice.

"Cheating?" spluttered his mum. "It's not cheating – it's survival. She who dares wins! It's a jungle out there, son."

Indiana hustled his parents away as quickly as possible.

Next, they came to the cake stall. Mr Brown's eyes lit up. There were enough strawberry slices, treacle tarts, chocolate-chip cookies, flapjacks and fairy cakes to feed a half-starved hippo.

"Indi, you should have told me about this," Mr Brown said. "I could have knocked up some of my muffins!"

"Dad, I don't think—" Indiana began. But he was interrupted by Mrs Turner, the teacher running the stall.

"A keen chef, eh, Mr Brown?" she asked.

Mr Brown smiled. "Absolutely," he replied. "You can't beat wholesome food, can you?"

"You can't," she agreed. "Try these butterfly cakes, they're delicious."

Mr Brown peered at them. "Ah, shame, I thought you meant *real* butterflies," he said.

50p Each

The teacher gave him a strange look but Mr Brown didn't notice. "Have you ever tried a bushtucker biscuit?" he went on. "That's what *I* call delicious."

"Dad, don't," Indiana said urgently. The
less Dad said about his awful bushtucker
biscuits, the better!

But Indiana's dad wasn't listening.

"A bushtucker biscuit," he said, "is so good, it positively wriggles in the mouth. Anything from the garden will do. A worm, a beetle, or a slug, for more of a melt-in-the-mouth texture..."

The teacher's red cheeks turned white, and then a vile shade of green. She ran off, one hand clapped to her mouth.

Mr Brown watched her disappear in amazement. "What did I say?" he asked.

Next, Mrs Brown had a go on the buzzer game. "Compared to rattlesnake-wrestling, this is nothing. I've got nerves of steel," she said, as she won a blue teddy bear.

Then Mr Brown tried the hoopla. "I've lassooed a few wildebeest in my time," he boasted, as he won a huge fluffy duck. "You know what they say – he who dares wins!"

Indiana bought a water pistol and a couple of old annuals. He jumped with Joe on the bouncy castle, and bought a raffle ticket. He was starting to enjoy himself after all.

At the end of the day, the head teacher, Mrs Bullneck, gathered everyone to call out the prize numbers for the raffle.

"The winner of this beautiful china doll is...number 73," she announced.

Joe groaned. "I don't believe it," he said, holding up his ticket. "That's my number!"

Everyone laughed as Joe went up to get his doll. Everyone except Joe, that is.

"The winner of this totally terrific TV set is...number 38," droned Mrs Bullneck.

But Indiana had stopped listening. Out of the corner of one eye, he could see his mum bouncing on the bouncy castle.

Out of the corner of his other eye, he could see his dad juggling coconuts at the coconut shy.

Joe elbowed him suddenly. "Indi – you're number 128, aren't you?" Indiana blinked. What had he won? Something good, by the sound of it. Lots of people were clapping. With wobbly legs, he walked up.

"We hope you and your family enjoy this, Indiana," said Mrs Bullneck. "Ladies and gentleman – our star prize has gone to Indiana Brown!"

Everyone clapped. Indiana felt faint. Star prize? What was she talking about?

Mrs Bullneck passed him a gold envelope.

"Thank you," Indiana said. A holiday? His parents were going to love this! "Thank you very much."

Indiana found his mum and dad at the *Guess The Name Of The Stick Insect* stall.

"How do you spell 'Hercules'?" his dad was asking.

Indiana waved the envelope in the air. "I've won a prize," he told them. "A holiday!"

"A *holiday*?" echoed his mum.

Indiana opened the golden envelope.

"It's a trip to..." he started. Then he smiled. "Oh, wow. Brilliant!"

"Where?" Dad asked. "South America?"

"India?" Mum said, crossing her fingers.

"It's better than that," beamed Indiana.
"A week at the Boggy Beach Holiday Camp!"
Dad frowned. "Is that in Borneo?"
Mum looked thoughtful. "We'll have to get some new jabs done."

Indiana laughed. "It's not *abroad*," he told them. "We don't have to fly there. We don't need passports or vaccinations. It's in this country. A seaside holiday!"

Indiana was so excited. He wouldn't have
to worry about creepy-crawlies in his
sleeping bag. He wouldn't have to eat weird
food, or watch out for dangerous animals.
Best of all, there would be loads of other
children he could make friends with.

Mr and Mrs Brown weren't quite so excited. It sounded rather *safe* for their liking. No mountains or rainforest? No sharks or poisonous snakes? Still, they were sure they'd find *something* dangerous to do there.

After a few days at Boggy Beach, Indiana felt happier than he had done in ages. He had played football with his new mates. He'd swum thirty lengths of the pool without stopping. And he'd had sausages and chips every single night. It was the best holiday of his life!

To everyone's surprise, Mr and Mrs Brown were having fun, too. Sure, there wasn't much exploring to do. But there were other things. Things they had never even dreamed of doing before.

Mr Brown had entered the knobbly knees contest, and won third prize. He said it was his finest moment since he'd discovered a small island off the coast of Brazil.

Mrs Brown had warbled her way through
seven songs at the karaoke contest. She didn't
win a prize but she said it was the bravest
thing she'd done since tackling a tiger
in Thailand.

They had both attended the balloon-bending class that morning. Mr Brown had made a balloon flamingo. Mrs Brown had made a...well, she was very pleased with it, anyway, whatever it was.

"Isn't it lucky you won that prize in the raffle, Indi?" Indiana's mum and dad said as they walked back to their chalet to get changed for the banana bouncing contest. "We never knew you could have so much fun right here, in this country."

"So you mean..."
Indiana took
a deep breath.
"We might have a
holiday like this again?
Maybe even with Nan?"

Mr and Mrs Brown
looked at each other.
"I don't see why not,"
Mrs Brown said.
"I mean, you can't do
karaoke in ancient
temples, can you?"

Mr Brown nodded.
"And I'm sure I can
win first prize at the
Mr Knobbly Knees
contest next time,"
he said.

Indiana felt as if his whole face was one huge smile. He smiled at his mum. He smiled at his dad. And as he looked at them, he realised something. For the first time, they actually looked quite normal. Just like all the other mums and dads. It was *great*!

Later that day, after coming third in the lilo-racing tournament, Indiana went to look for Mum and Dad. His *normal* mum and dad! He chuckled to himself as he wondered what they might be doing.

Maybe Dad would be discussing knobbly knees with the other dads. Maybe Mum would be swapping balloon-bending tips with the other mums. Or maybe...

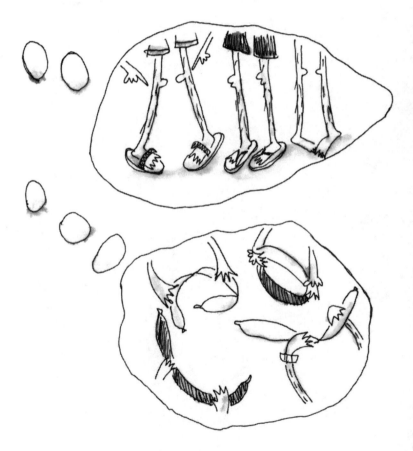

Indiana stopped in his tracks. There in
front of him was... Oh, *no*!

Mr Brown was wearing a grass skirt, with
a pair of bongo drums around his neck. Mrs
Brown had on a wet suit with a snorkel,
mask and flippers.

"Mum, Dad, what are you *doing*?"
Indiana hissed, looking around in case any of
his new friends were nearby.

His mum beamed at him. "We're
giving a talk on our adventures," she said.
"Your dad's going to do the tribal dance of
Hula-Bula."

Indiana looked at his dad in horror.

"And your mum's going to tell everyone how she wrestled with that shark in the South Seas," Mr Brown said proudly. "She's going to demonstrate with a member of the audience. And we've got that video of you growing up in the jungle, too!"

"What, that video where I've got no clothes on?" Indiana groaned. He felt sick. Just as he'd thought they had changed for the better, they had become worse than ever!

FRIGHTFUL FAMILIES

WRITTEN BY SUE MONGREDIEN • ILLUSTRATED BY TERESA MURFIN

Explorer Trauma	1 84362 563 6
Headmaster Disaster	1 84362 564 4
Millionaire Mayhem	1 84362 565 2
Clown Calamity	1 84362 566 0
Popstar Panic	1 84362 567 9
Football-mad Dad	1 84362 568 7
Chef Shocker	1 84362 569 5
Astronerds	1 84362 570 9

All priced at £8.99

*

Frightful Families are available from all good book shops, or can be ordered
direct from the publisher: Orchard Books, PO BOX 29, Douglas IM99 1BQ
Credit card orders please telephone 01624 836000
or fax 01624 837033 or visit our Internet site: www.wattspub.co.uk
or e-mail: bookshop@enterprise.net for details.

To order please quote title, author and ISBN
and your full name and address.
Cheques and postal orders should be made payable to 'Bookpost plc.'
Postage and packing is FREE within the UK
(overseas customers should add £1.00 per book).
Prices and availability are subject to change.

Indiana hugged her back. "Of course
I am," he said. "With those knees, Dad,
I reckon you're in with a good chance.
Anyway, what is it you always say?
He who dares wins!"

Suddenly, Indiana found that he was laughing too. They were never going to change *that* much, were they? Normal? Fat chance. They were completely bonkers! But he still loved them.

Indiana's mum put her arm around him. "Sorry, love. We couldn't resist it. Are you going to come to cheer us on in this competition, or what?" she asked.